LESSONS FROM A SOUTHERN Mother

Bilingual Edition

Written by Alex Beene
Illustrations by Danny Martin

HILLIARD PRESS

LESSONS FROM A
SOUTHERN
Mother

Bilingual Edition

Written by Alex Beene
Illustrations by Danny Martin

In Loving Memory of
Deidra Hilliard Beene

My mother was the one who taught me all of the lessons in
this book. While she was taken from this world far too soon,
her legacy will continue on in the pages of this story and in the
phenomenal work she did. She was loved by friends, family,
and co-workers for her tireless dedication to education and the
improvement of her local community. Her spirit continues to
shine through in the many lives of the people she touched.

Forward

When I first met Alex, he expressed the one quality I loved: hope. He had hope for mankind and for those needing a future. He willfully shared how he desired to help our children. These qualities are often hidden in the younger generation, but Alex was willing to share his expertise to help them achieve their life goals, even when many had no desire to have a goal. I wondered where this burning desire to help others came from. I soon learned. It was from his mother.

Each morning, we open our eyes to a new day, a day of many certainties and endless possibilities. How we view each new day and how our life experiences have touched us will shape the bright horizon we see. We will all witness life through our own reality. Our family, friends, the people we will meet, and the conversations we will share will teach us many valuable lessons.

A child growing up in this world can be guided by those who open the window of opportunity or by those shading and covering reality only allowing a narrow view of this life. How do our children face the realities of an often confusing, ever-changing world? This world often displays the imperfections and doubts of a curious mankind. How can we assist our children in making a difference by challenging this world as we know it?

Alex introduces us to such a person in this book. She is a woman, a mother who grew up in the South at a very different time. She is full of grace and charm; however, deep inside she has a burning desire and inner resolve to change the past as she learned it to be. She has seen the poor, the needy, and those needing help in her community. She has witnessed the insensitivity of those who often surround her. She has experienced the lack of desire for the preservation of a rich heritage. The intolerance of others has invaded even her innermost circle of friends and family. This is and was her life.

She has chosen to challenge the misunderstanding of this life to many by sharing lessons of insight given to her son. He is beginning to embark upon his life journey of learning. The first day of school holds nothing but promise for him. She shares her lens of life through a very different window. Her son experiences his mother's lessons through a sphere of hope, love, and endless possibilities of what can make this world a much better place. Her desire is for the future to be better because her son will be a part of change. There is still hope.

The challenge for the young son is to embark upon a life of learning the real lessons of life. Those lessons are beautifully described in this book. I can only imagine the life's lessons Alex and his mother shared.

Dr. Charlotte Fisher

This book is dedicated to the mothers of the world. For as long as there are mothers, there will always be new lessons to be learned.

本書は、世界中すべてのお母さんに捧げられたものです。お母さんたちが世界にいる限り、子供らは新しい知恵を得ることができるのです。

"Jack, hurry up! I don't want you to be late for your first day of school," his mother Virginia yelled. Hearing his mother's call, he ran quickly down the stairs.

「ジャック、いそぎなさい。はじめての　がっこうで　ちこくしたら　ダメでしょ」　おかあさんの　バージニアは　おおきなこえで　いいました。こえを　きいた　ジャックは　かいだんを　かけおります。

"Straighten your collar a bit," his mother said. "Have you got everything you need?" Jack nodded, and the two walked out the door and toward the car.

「さあ、えりを　なおして」　「わすれものは　ない？」　ジャックは　うなずき、ふたりは　そとにでて　くるまに　のりこみます。

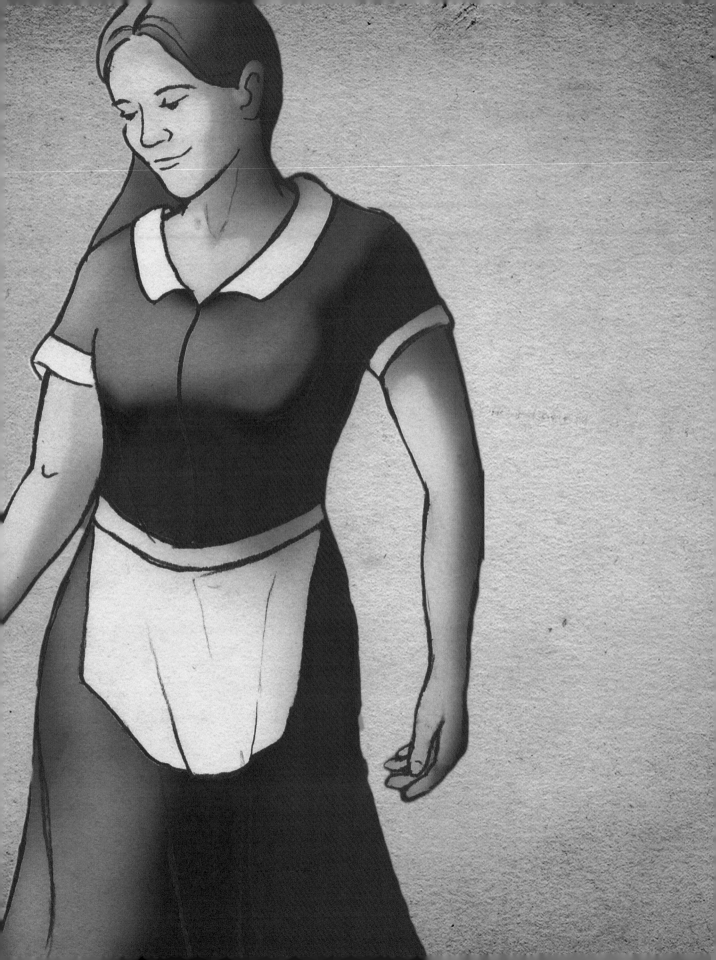

It was an important day for Jack. He was going to attend kindergarten for the first time. As his mother buckled him in, she noticed him shaking a bit. He was very nervous.

そのひは　ジャックにとって　とても　たいせつな　ひでした。はじめての　がっこうだったのです。　おかあさんは　シートベルトを　しめながら、すこし　ジャックが　ふるえているのに　きづきました。　ジャックは　ひどく　きんちょうしていたのです。

"You have nothing to be afraid of, son," his mother told him as she climbed into the front seat.

"You're going to have a ton of fun."

おかあさんは　「なにも　こわがることなんて　ないのよ」　と　うんてんせきに　すわりながら　いいました。「がっこうは　とっても　たのしいところよ」

Jack finally spoke up.
"How do you know?" he asked.
"I don't know if any of the other
kids will like me. And what if the
teacher asks a question and I don't
know the right answer?"

「そんなの　わからないや」　や
っと　ジャックは　くちを　ひら
き　いいました。　「いじめっこ
が　いるかもしれないし、せんせ
いの　しつもんに　こたえられな
かったら　どうするの？」

"Oh, honey, you shouldn't be worried. You'll do fine. Just remember a few things," Virginia began to tell her son.

「ジャック、しんぱいしないで。だいじょうぶよ。でも、いまから いうことだけは ちゃんと おぼえておきなさい」おかあさんは ジャックに いいました。

"If you see classmates needing help, lend them a hand. We all need someone to lift us up from time to time when we fall down."

「こまっているこが　いれば　そのこを　たすけてあげなさい。なにかに　つまずいて　おきあがれないときには、だれだって　ほかのひとからの　たすけが　ひつようでしょう」

Acts of kindness in the wake of Hurricane Katrina helped promote dignity in a time of chaos. New Orleans, Louisiana, 2005.

"Make sure you always present yourself as a dedicated, persistent person. You want to preserve your character and your working area. Clean up after yourself. Your teacher will appreciate that."

「ひたむきで　ねばりづよく　ありなさい。こせいを　もって　しっかりと　べんきょうを　しなさい。せいりせいとんを　しなさい。そうすると　きっと　せんせいに　かんしゃされるはず」

Downtown Savannah, Georgia, is celebrated world-wide for its beauty and preservation of southern heritage.

"Be kind and understanding to others, even if they're different in thoughts or appearance from you. The best people are always the most accepting."

「じぶんと　ちがう　かんがえや　みための　ひとにも　やさしく　しんせつにすること。ひろい　こころを　もつひとは　このよで　いちばん　すばらしいひと」

The statue of James Meredith walking into the campus at Ole Miss, as the first African-American student, commemorates the efforts of those who strove to create educational opportunities for all citizens in the South.

"Never be afraid to learn new things. The best students always explore the unknown and broaden their horizons."

「いつも　あたらしいことを　まなびなさい。ゆうとうせいは　いつも　まわりを　みわたして　じぶんが　しらないことが　ないかと　さがしているのよ」

The NASA sites in Houston, Texas; Cape Canaveral, Florida; and Huntsville, Alabama, have been a source of wonder and discovery since 1958.

"Always speak up for what you know to be right, even if it isn't popular with your classmates. Speaking the truth will help you gain the friends you want in your life. Trust me."

「みんなが　はんたいしても　じぶんが　ただしいと　しんじるのなら、　そのかんがえを　つきとおすこと。　じぶんに　しょうじきな　ひとには、ほんとうの　ともだちが　できるの。ほんとうよ」

Dr. Martin Luther King Jr. was not only born and raised in the South, but forever changed it. His words of truth and courage are still echoing across the world.

"Oh yes, and even when you have a bad day, remember to look for bright spots. Darkness may appear to be all around you, but there's always a glimmer of light that shines somewhere. Find and cherish it."

「それとね、もし いやなことが あっても そのとき なにか ひとつだけでも いいことを みつけることがたいせつ。まっくらやみに ひとりで いるような きが する かも しれないけれど、いつも どこかに ひとすじの ひかりが さしこんでいるはず。それを みつけて そのひかりに かんしゃしなさい」

The survivor tree, which endured the Oklahoma City bombing of 1995, has become a symbol of hope and strength. Its branches reach higher each day.

Jack had a big smile on his face. "Thanks, Mom. I'll try to remember all that."

ジャックは　おおきな　えがおで　いいました。「おかあさん、ありがとう。おぼえとくね」

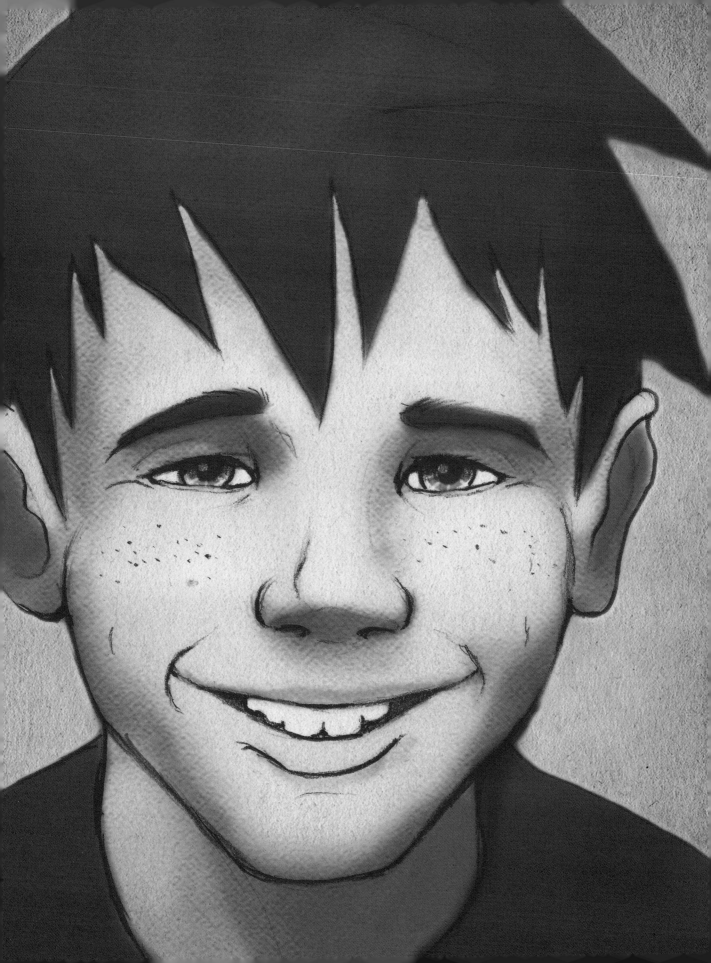

As Virginia pulled up to the school building, Jack started to unbuckle his belt. "Where did you learn all that stuff? You must have been a lot of places and met a lot of people to know so much."

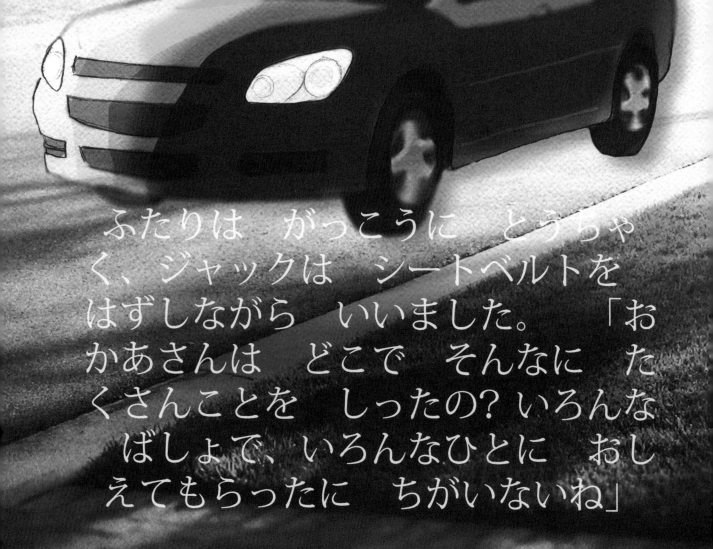

ふたりは　がっこうに　とうちゃく、ジャックは　シートベルトをはずしながら　いいました。「おかあさんは　どこで　そんなに　たくさんことを　しったの? いろんなばしょで、いろんなひとに　おしえてもらったに　ちがいないね」

"Son, I learned all those lessons from the South and its people," his mother said with a wide grin. "You'll experience all these traits in time, too. Just hold on to what I taught you."

「ジャック、おかあさんは　なんぶしゅっしんの　かしこいひとから　ちえを　まなんだのよ」　バージニアは　ニコッと　わらって　いいました。「おおきくなったら　きっと　あなたも　けいけんするはず。　いま　おかあさんが　いったことは、ぜんぶ　おぼえておきなさい」

"I will, Momma!" Jack yelled. He walked to the front doors of the school in a good mood. He'd have a great first day thanks to the lessons his mother taught him.

「やくそくする！」　ジャックは さけび、　じょうきげんで　がっこうの　もんを　くぐりました。おかあさんに　かけてもらった　ことばの　おかげで、ジャックは　そのひ　がっこうで　すばらしい　いちにちを　すごせたことでしょう。

Our Team

Alex Beene is an author, journalist, and educator from Tennessee. A constant traveler and advocate for global human rights, he's been to over 20 countries and is certified in English as a Second Language instruction from the University of California, Los Angeles. He has been named one of the top Forty under 40 leaders in West Tennessee by the *Jackson Sun* and is a constant contributor to charitable projects in the region that promote community development and the arts. His work has been featured in various publications throughout the Southeastern United States, where he received his bachelor's and master's degrees in Journalism from the University of Mississippi.

Danny Martin is an illustrator, graphic designer, and adventurer born and raised in St. Petersburg, Florida. Upon graduating from Freed-Hardeman University in Henderson, Tennessee, he began working with Bramblett Group, a creative agency that allowed him to expand his talents. His work spans multiple mediums, including fine art, video animation, and graphic design. A philanthropist at heart, Danny's passion is using his art to promote the welfare of others. When he's not creating, the Austin, Texas, resident will most likely be found playing ultimate frisbee, climbing a tree, or enjoying the park with his dog, Dakota.

Dr. Charlotte Fisher is a native of Tipton County of Tennessee. She is a career educator in the local school system. Charlotte is a wife of over thirty years, mother of five, and the grandmother of six. She is actively involved in the community and her local church. Growing up in rural Tennessee during the 60s and 70s, her journey through life has carried her through many of the experiences shared in *Lessons from a Southern Mother*. Her career and family choices have allowed her to teach many lessons to children. She strives every day to help others be the best they can be and remember to never, never give up.

Joshua Sells is a photographer from Tennessee. He runs Joshua Sells Photography, one of the most in-demand local media businesses in the area. He currently attends Freed-Hardeman University.

Our Bilingual Team

Jorge Luis Perez Valery is a journalist from Venezuela. An anchor for various programs on Globovision, the nation's primary news television channel, he worked as a producer at Globovision's International News Desk. He also worked on a project for Vale TV, a science TV station managed by the Venezuelan Catholic Church. Currently, he is a correspondent for Claro Colombia.

Jose Urzua is a Spanish translator originally from California. He has been involved in numerous projects that looked to merge Spanish culture into the Western world. He currently resides in Henderson, Tennessee, where he attends Freed-Hardeman University.

Anthony Yuen is a native of Hattiesburg, Mississippi, and a current resident of Washington, D.C. Proficient in Mandarin Chinese, Anthony works in the field of international affairs and business, specializing in East Asian affairs and Sino-American relations. He received his B.A. in International Studies and Chinese from the University of Mississippi and his M.S. in Foreign Service from Georgetown University.

Kumiko Murakami Campos is a professional photographer and a writer from Osaka, Japan. Landed in the United States at the age of 18, she graduated from Kansai Gaidai Hawaii College and the University of Northern Colorado. She has a bachelor's degree in Visual Arts majoring in Photographic Imaging. Hopping throughout the country and contributing pictures and stories to many different publications, she is currenty residing in North Texas and enjoying shooting high school football games on Friday nights.

Special Thanks

We simply wouldn't have been able to complete this book without the love of the individuals listed in this section. Our utmost thanks to these people who not only financially contributed to this endeavor, but also offered up constant inspiration and support. We love and appreciate all of you.

Alex P. Vega

Amber and Amelia Jewell Guthrie

Amy Warden West

Andrew Hart

Angelia White Haltom

Anthony Beene

Aphiwe Campbell Harston

Bill and Ann Vernon

Blake, Lauren, and Brayden White

Bob Martin

Brenda Keller

Brooxie Carlton

Carolyn Schlemmer

Catherine Servati

Chad and Jennifer Davis

Chris Bright

Clayton Martin

Clint and Katherine Rosenblatt

Chris, Alana, William, and Haley Vernon

Cooper Reves

Dalton Sheffield

David Hopper

David, Amy, and Eli Ray

David, April, Elam, and Haley Kate Dierks

Deryl and Vicki Hilliard

Diane Martin

DJ Norton

Donald and Carolyn Gaines

Drew Wilkerson and Mallory Blasingame

Ethel Young-Minor

Emily Hunt Johnson

Erica Bell

Farhan Manjiyani

Gabby Bernstein

Heather Stewart

Horace and Mary Sue Beene

Jack and Lola Hilliard

Janet Mclemore

Jay, Jessa, June, Jack, and Jonas Sexton

Jenilyn, Garrett, and Grayson Sipes

Jennifer Rose Adams

Jeremy Gatson

Jerr Clarke

Joe Atkins

Joe Smiley

Joe, Jessica, and Addison Lee Wright

John, Emily, Samantha, and Juliette Darnell

Jordan Bach

Joseph and Palmer Williams

Judy Martin

Kara Waddell Tapp

Kate and Ellen Meacham

Kathleen Donnenworth

Kathleen Wickham

Kenny and Sandy King

L Kasimu Harris

Landy Fuqua

Lee Pipkin

Leigh Ann Alexander Skaggs

Lorinda Krhut

Lynn Russell

Maleia M. Evans

Mark and Rosemary Hilliard

Mark-Aaron, Celeste, Charlie, and Isaac Hilliard

Mark Dolan

Mary Collins, Meghan, and William Tyler Massey

Mickey and Gay Crosby

Morgan Jones

Nancy Dupont

Neil, Mary Ann, Katie, and Jack Griffith

Patrick Grimes

Phillip and Leslie Carpenter

Reid and Callie Wesson

Rob Carpenter and Haley Crosby

Sammy, Lisa, and Jacob Beene

Sarah Conrad

Shelby Jumper

Shelia Carter Viar

Stephen and Carrie Sells

Stewart and Betsy Hood

Susan Edmonds

Tammy Smith Hall

Tate Crosby

Taylor McGraw

Tiffany Flippin

Ty, Rachel, Camryn, and Travis Connor

Virginia Grimes

Warner and Katelyn Russell

William, Myers, and Annie Carpenter

Willie and Dixie Spencer

Winsor Yuan